Han's friend rushed up. "How you doing, you old pirate?" Lando shouted with a laugh. "Let me show you around my little operation here. City on top. Gas mine below. Clever, huh?"

"You always were," said Han as they entered the main building. "But what does the Empire think of your mining setup? You worried they might close you down?"

"Well, to tell the truth, I was. I really was."

"So what happened?"

"I made a deal."

Lando threw open a door. Waiting on the other side was one of Jabba the Hutt's bounty hunters.

And Darth Vader!

C L A S S I C

STAR WARS™

The Empire Strikes Back™

CLASSIC

STAR WARS™

The Empire Strikes Back™

Adapted by Larry Weinberg
from the screenplay by
Leigh Brackett and Lawrence Kasdan

Story by George Lucas

Reed Books Children's Publishing

First published in Great Britain by Reed Books Children's Publishing
Michelin House, 81 Fulham Road, London SW3 6RB
and Auckland, Melbourne, Singapore and Toronto
®, TM & © 1985, 1996 Lucasfilm Ltd. (LFL).

ISBN 0 7497 2949 X

1 3 5 7 9 10 8 6 4 2

Printed and bound in Great Britain
by Cox & Wyman Ltd., Reading, Berkshire

PROLOGUE

Long ago, in a galaxy far, far away, an evil empire ruled. A Rebel Alliance sprang up to fight it. But the fight was long and hard.

Luke Skywalker was a young Rebel hero. He blew the Empire's battle station, the Death Star, into space dust. For a time this saved the Rebels.

Then the Empire grew strong again. The Imperial fleet drove the Rebels from their base. And Darth Vader hounded them across the galaxy.

At last the Rebels found a new hiding place. It was a planet of snow and ice...

CHAPTER ONE

Luke galloped to the top of the frozen hill on his snow lizard. Something was dropping down out of the sky. It made a hole in the ice. What was it?

"I hope it's only a meteor," he thought. "But it could be an Imperial space probe, looking for us. Better check it out."

Luke dug his boots into the animal's sides. But the tauntaun would not move. Something had scared it. Luke looked behind him quickly. A huge snow creature reared up above him. Its great paw lashed out at Luke's face. Lights exploded before his eyes. And then he fell into darkness.

It was nighttime when Luke came to. He staggered to his feet. He was shivering. Weak. He looked around. His snow lizard was gone.

The night was bitterly cold and growing worse. It would be a long, long walk back to base. *If* he could find it. But if he stood there much longer, the wind would turn his blood to ice.

"Start walking," he told himself. "Keep moving or you'll die."

Everyone was very busy back at the new Rebel base. They were too busy to notice that Commander Skywalker still had not come back. But the little droid Artoo noticed. He had been watching and waiting all day. Now he beeped his worries to his friend Threepio.

"Well, why didn't you say so before?" said the tall droid. "I'll go and find Princess Leia right away."

Threepio hurried from one ice tunnel to another. Finally he found the princess in the hangar section. She was standing beside Han Solo as he worked on his smuggling ship. They were arguing.

"Look!" said Han. "I've helped you Rebels all I can. Soon as Chewie and I fix the *Falcon*, I'm leaving. Got to go square things with a guy who's after my head."

"Always worrying about yourself!" Leia shot back at him.

"That's me all over, Your Highness. I got this selfish thing about staying alive. And you don't know anybody like Jabba the Hutt."

"Princess Leia!" Threepio cried as he hurried over. "Captain Solo!"

"You stay out of this!" they both snapped.

"Listen, Han!" said Leia. "You know very well that we need you here."

"Why don't you just admit you're waiting for a good-bye kiss?" Han said with a grin.

"From *you?* I'd rather kiss a…a Wookiee!"

Chewie looked down from the *Falcon*'s wing and growled.

"Oh, please listen, somebody!" cried Threepio. "Master Luke hasn't returned from his patrol. He's still out there!"

"What?" shouted Han. "Why didn't you say so in the first place!" He rushed to one of the snow lizards and threw a saddle on it.

"You can't go out there at night!" warned a Rebel officer. "Your tauntaun will freeze to death before the first marker."

"That's exactly what I need," Han called back as he rode out of the ice cave. "Encouraging advice!"

Meanwhile, Luke had lost his way in the dark. The wind whipped through his clothes. And he could no longer feel his feet as they moved beneath him.

Then all at once they *weren't* moving. The snowy ground came rushing up at him. He had fallen face first.

Then he heard a voice. "Luke," it said gently. "Luke."

"Ben?"

The boy lifted his head. Before him on the ice stood old Ben Kenobi. Ben was the Jedi general who had died on the Death Star. Vader had killed him.

"I must be seeing things," Luke thought.

"They say it happens before you freeze to death."

"Luke, listen to me…"

"Ben!" The boy tried to reach out. But his arms wouldn't move.

"Listen," said Ben Kenobi. "You will go to the Dagobah system. There you will learn from Yoda to become a true Jedi. He is the Master who taught me when I was young."

Again Luke reached out, but the vision was gone. Then he passed out.

CHAPTER TWO

Han's lizard moved quickly over the ice. The wind was behind it, pushing it on. But the cold air was tiring the racing beast.

The tauntaun reached the place where Luke lay upon the ice. Then its legs crumpled underneath it.

Han leaped free of the dying beast and rushed to his friend. The barest whisper of breath came from Luke's nostrils. He was still alive!

"Got to warm him up!" thought Han.

But with what? There was no shelter anywhere.

Han's gaze fell on his tauntaun. It would be warm inside the beast's belly. What if he were to open the animal up and put his friend inside?

The whole idea made Han feel sick to his stomach. But he knew he had to do it—or watch Luke die. Han took his friend's lightsaber and cut.

The bitter night went on. And on. At last the sun began to rise. Dawn glowed red over the ice planet. It brought enough warmth to make the transmitter in Han's pocket start to work again.

The voice of one of the Rebel pilots came on. He was searching for Han and Luke in a snowspeeder.

Minutes later the pilot appeared. Han's

half-frozen face twisted into a grin. "So nice of you to drop by."

Soon they were racing back to the base in the ice caves. As soon as they arrived, Luke was taken to sick bay.

Princess Leia had been waiting for them. She was worried.

"He's all right," Han told her. "Just needs a little rest. But he was saying something on the way back. Something about a meteor coming down."

Leia nodded. "We've just picked it up on our scopes. That's no meteor. It's a droid. And it's sending signals back into space. Using an Imperial code."

"Meaning what?"

"Vader's found us," she said. "His fleet will be here in no time."

"How ready for a fight are we?"

The princess looked grim. "Our overhead

energy shield is completed. This means we can stop them from bombing us. But they can land all the troops they want just past the shield. Then they can sweep in under it and wipe us out. So we've got to get away from here. Only there isn't much time."

"Gee," said Han. "I'm really glad I asked."

Far across the galaxy, Darth Vader stepped onto the bridge of his command ship.

"Admiral," he said, speaking to one of the officers, "you have found something, have you not?"

A chill went up the officer's spine. The report had just arrived. How could Vader know about it so quickly?

"Yes, my lord," replied the admiral. "There seem to be human life forms on a planet in the Hoth system. But it is too early to be sure. They could be explorers or—"

"That's it," said Vader. "That is the Rebel

base. And Skywalker is with them. Alert the fleet. We shall go there at once."

He left the bridge as swiftly as he had come.

CHAPTER THREE

Back on Hoth, Luke would not stay in bed. The pilots were all counting on him. He raced out of sick bay as a loudspeaker boomed.

"Attention! Attention! Imperial Star Destroyers coming out of hyperspace in Sector Four!"

"Close the energy shield!" Princess Leia ordered. "And give it all the power we've got!" She turned to her officers just as Luke ran up.

"Vader's going to land troopers," she said. "He'll send them after our energy towers first. That way they can knock down our shield. We're going to fly most of our people out of here. But you've got to protect the towers until our transports can get away safely."

"May the Force be with us all," one of the officers said. Then they rushed off to their commands.

Luke was the first one to his armored snowspeeder. The other pilots leaped into theirs and prepared to lift off. Then the loudspeaker blared again.

"This is Forward Post Three. The Imperials are landing." The voice grew shaky. "Only they're not soldiers! They're like animals! Big as mountains!"

The man's voice grew even shakier. "They're burning and crushing everything in their way! Our lasers are only bouncing off them!"

"Let's go!" Luke called into his comlink. The little fleet he commanded sped out of the caves.

The Rebel pilots were all brave. But their guns were useless against the Walkers. Luke knew he had to think of something—fast. Or the transports wouldn't have time to get away.

"Use your harpoons and tow ropes!" he told his pilots. "Wind them around the Walkers' legs. Trip them."

The pilot called Zev peeled off on an attack run. His ship shot past a Walker's head. Luke watched as the huge head turned. Then he saw the laser bolt. The first shot missed, but Luke knew the next one wouldn't. In a moment Zev's ship would be burned to ashes.

It was too late to warn him. There was only one thing to do. Luke threw his speeder into a climb. He blasted at the Walker, and the machine's great head swung back his way. Its lasers shot out at him. His speeder burst into flames.

Luke leaped away just before it blew up. Quickly, he fired his harpoon at the Walker's belly. He caught the rope and hung on. Then he began to climb. There was a tiny hatch above him. Swiftly, he cut a hole in it with his lightsaber. Then he threw a small land mine inside.

He was only halfway down the rope when the Walker exploded. The huge machine began to fall. Luke fell with it.

* * *

Things were going very badly at the base. Enemy fire struck again and again. There was a danger of a great cave-in. It could trap them all. And it could destroy the ships that were needed for escape.

Princess Leia turned to her general. "We can't hold out any longer. I want all our soldiers back from the fighting. Get them into the transport ships. Have them make a run for it."

Her officers begged her to get on one of the ships. But she wouldn't listen. It was her duty to make sure everyone else escaped first. One after another, the ships flew off without her.

"They're getting away!" she thought. "Thank the Force!"

Soon the Walkers were storming the caves. Enemy troops came with them. Their gunfire rocked the tunnels. The walls and roofs of ice began to crack. Great chunks broke off and fell around Leia.

All at once, Han was at her side. He grabbed her by the hand. "Come on! Let's get to my ship!"

"Wait for me!" shouted Threepio. "Doesn't anybody care about a droid?"

CHAPTER FOUR

Luke had fallen clear of the destroyed
Walker. The battle had passed him by.
When he came to, he saw the *Falcon* climb-
ing into the sky.

The Imperials were not close enough to see
him. Quietly, he slipped away to the hangar
where his X-wing spacecraft was kept.

Artoo had been waiting for him. The little
droid beeped with relief at seeing him. Luke
climbed into his ship and started the

engines. He remembered again his vision on the ice.

"You will go to the Dagobah system," Ben Kenobi had told him. "There you will learn from Yoda to become a true Jedi…"

The *Falcon* hadn't made a clean getaway from the ice planet. Enemy TIE fighters and a big destroyer had spotted it. Now they were closing in from behind.

Leia was worried. It wasn't only *her* life she was thinking about. Or Han's. Or Chewie's. The Rebels were counting on her. They would be waiting for her on the other side of the galaxy. She *had* to link up with her transports.

"Han!" she cried. "Why aren't we jumping to lightspeed?"

"You really wanna know?" he snapped. "Tell her, Chewie!"

The Wookiee let out an angry howl.

"Is he saying the hyperdrive isn't working?" she asked.

"That's it, Your Highness!"

"Oh, no!" cried Threepio. "They're firing at us. We're doomed! Doomed!"

"Hold tight!" shouted Han. He threw the *Falcon* into a steep dive. "Maybe this'll work. Then again, maybe not!"

There was a loud crash and the ship shook. Then another crash made it plunge. And a third sent it into a spin.

Leia rushed to the cockpit window. Huge chunks of rock were whizzing by in all directions. "Asteroids! You've flown us into an asteroid belt!"

Han's eyes widened. Two giant rocks were coming at each other. And the *Falcon* was in the middle! At the last second Han threw the *Falcon* into a climb. The asteroids collided.

They exploded like bombs just beneath the *Falcon*.

Now the ship began to rattle and shake. "This bucket's going to come apart if I don't repair it right away," Han thought.

There was a huge asteroid nearby. Diving low over it, Han saw the entrance to a cave. It was large enough to fly into. He cut the ship's engines. The *Falcon* glided like a bird into the pitch-black opening.

CHAPTER FIVE

Darth Vader didn't want to hear excuses from his commanders. He wanted the *Falcon*—and its passengers—captured. "They are still alive," he told his officers. "Keep searching the asteroid belt." Then he swiftly left the bridge. His own master was calling him.

He went into a chamber where no one but he might enter. Out of the air, the giant image of the Emperor rose before him.

Vader bowed down. Then he lifted his head. Above him was a face that might have belonged to Death itself.

The Emperor spoke. "There has been a great disturbance in the Force. Kenobi is gone. But we have a new enemy. Young Luke Skywalker. He could destroy us. We must rid ourselves of him. Quickly."

For a moment Darth Vader was silent. "But, my Master," he said. "What if this boy could be turned to the dark side of the Force?"

The Emperor grew thoughtful. "He would be a powerful ally. But can it be done?"

Vader knelt again. "You may leave it to me, Master. He will join us or die."

The Emperor passed a ghostly hand over his commander-in-chief. Then he faded away.

* * *

At just about the same time, Luke was try-
ing to land on Dagobah. The clouds above
the planet were thick. Too thick to see
through. So Luke came down blind. His ship
landed right in the middle of a swamp.

Luke waded to shore. He could see nothing in the fog. Nothing but the dark, twisted
shape of jungle trees.

"This place gives me the creeps, Artoo. I
feel like we're being—"

"Being what?" croaked a strange, froglike
voice.

"Watched!" Luke spun around with his
blaster.

"Away put your weapon! I mean no
harm."

Luke stared at a tiny creature who was
standing on a log. It was smaller than
Artoo. It had long ears and a pointy head. It
was dressed in rags. And it seemed to be

Luke on his tauntaun.

Han Solo finds an Imperial probe droid
and destroys it.

The Rebels fight the Imperial walkers.

The Rebels escape
on the *Falcon*.

Stormtroopers, led by Darth Vader, invade
the Rebel base.

Luke escapes and
lands on Dagobah,
in search of Yoda.

"Artoo", says Luke, "stay and watch after the camp."

"I happen to be a nice man," Han tells Leia.

Yoda begins to teach Luke how to be
a true Jedi.

Yoda uses the Force to recover Luke's ship
from the swamp.

Han's old friend, Lando Calrissian,
offers safe haven at Cloud City.

But it's a trap!

A stormtrooper looks on as Han is prepared for the carbon freeze.

Darth Vader and Luke meet for
the first time.

Luke, Leia, and the droids rest,
safe at last with the Rebel fleet.

very old. Much too old to be dangerous.

"I'm looking for someone," Luke said.

The little creature's ears went up. It laughed. "*Looking?* Only looking? *Found* someone, you have. Hmmmm?"

"Well, that's true." Luke smiled. "But I mean a great warrior."

"Hmmmm? Wars not make one great."

"Well," said Luke, "his name is Yoda. He's a Jedi Master."

"Oho!" replied the creature. "Yoda! Hmmmm. Take you to him, I will. But now we must eat. Come."

But Luke was in a hurry. "Wait! There's no time for that!"

"No time to eat! What would become of the universe if there was no time to eat!" Laughing merrily, he led Luke to his tiny mud hut.

The boy had to duck to enter it. Then he

had to sit on the floor so he wouldn't bump against the ceiling. Then he had to wait *for-ever* while the creature cooked!

"Look!" Luke cried. "This is important! When can we go see Yoda?"

The old gnome turned away. "The boy has no patience," he said to himself. "I cannot teach him."

And then there was another voice in the room. A familiar voice. "He will learn patience as I did," said Ben Kenobi.

Luke's mouth fell open. "You! You're Yoda?"

The Jedi Master looked away. "He is not ready," he murmured.

Luke sprang to his feet. "Yoda! I *am* ready to be a Jedi. Ben, tell him!"

"Ready, is he?" snorted Yoda. "What knows he of ready? For eight hundred years I have trained Jedi. A Jedi must give all that is within him. He must have the most serious mind. But *this* one for a long time have I watched. All his life he has looked away to the future...to what was far away. Never his mind on where he was. On what he was doing. No! Adventure and excitement he wants. Humph! A Jedi wants not these things."

Suddenly he turned to Luke. "You are reckless!"

Yoda spoke the truth—and Luke knew it. All he wanted now was a chance to show that he *could* change. That he *would* give his heart and soul to becoming a real Jedi.

Yoda's voice softened as he spoke to Ben Kenobi. "He is too old to begin the training now."

"We have come this far," said Ben.

"Will he finish what he begins?"

"I will," said Luke. "And I promise I won't fail you. I'm not afraid."

Slowly Yoda turned to look at him. "You will be, young one. You will be…"

CHAPTER SIX

And so the training began. Day after day Yoda tied himself to Luke's back. "Run!" he would cry. "Faster! Faster! A Jedi's strength flows from the Force!"

Soon Luke was rushing along like the wind. Yoda taught him how to leap to great heights. How to climb as swiftly as any tree animal. How to find his way through the thickest fog. And how to make things move just by using his mind!

One day Luke was practicing on a rock when Artoo hurried over. The droid was beeping loudly. Luke followed it to the swamp where their X-wing fighter had landed.

"Oh, no!" he cried. "My ship has sunk completely. Now we'll never get it out."

"So sure are you?" said Yoda.

"Master, moving stones is one thing. This is different."

"No different!" Yoda shot back. "Only different in your mind. Use the Force!"

"All right, I'll give it a try."

"Try not!" Yoda shouted. "Do!"

Luke closed his eyes. He turned all his thoughts to the sunken ship. In his mind he saw it lifting out of the water. And slowly…slowly…the spacecraft began to rise out of the muck.

But now Luke's head was pounding. He

broke into a sweat. "Master," he panted. "It's too big!" Suddenly Luke let go.

Yoda watched the ship slip back under the murky water. He shook his head. "Size?" he asked. "What has size to do with it? Look at *me*. Judge me by *my* size, do you?"

Before Luke could reply, the Jedi Master closed his eyes. Then he lifted one arm toward the water.

Luke stared in amazement. The X-wing rose out of the water. Then it floated in the air! "I don't believe it!" cried Luke.

"That," said Yoda, "is why you fail."

The old teacher set the ship down on the shore and gazed at Luke. The boy had learned this lesson, he thought. But there was more...so much more he should be taught. Time. If only there were enough time...

* * *

Luke's friends also needed time—time to repair the *Falcon*. But there was something strange about the cavern where they had landed. The walls were dripping with water. And the ground was soft and sticky. Then all at once the whole place began to shake.

Leia was thrown to the ground. "The cave is collapsing!" she shouted.

"This is no cave!" yelled Han as he helped her up. Together, they rushed back into the ship. "It's a *mouth!*"

He gunned the engines. Then he headed straight for the entrance. Those rocks up ahead were no rocks, either. They were teeth. And they were closing! Threepio screamed. Chewie barked. At the last second the ship slipped through.

But once they were aloft, an Imperial Star Destroyer was on their tail. Han tried to make the jump to lightspeed. But the hyper-drive still wasn't working. There was only one thing left to do. He turned the *Falcon* around and headed straight for the enemy.

CHAPTER SEVEN

The captain of the destroyer stared at his viewscreen. What had happened to the tiny pirate craft that had dared to attack his ship? One minute it was there in front of him. Then it was gone!

The captain did not know that the *Falcon* was clinging to the back of his own ship. For hours Han kept it there. He waited until the great warship threw its garbage overboard. Then, hidden by the trash, Han released the *Falcon*'s magnetic clamps and flew the ship away!

Leia was proud of Han. Han was happy too. He thought they had escaped. He didn't see the small ship that was following them. It was not an Imperial ship but a pirate craft like his own.

Darth Vader had called in bounty hunters to help find the *Falcon*. One was a killer who worked for Jabba the Hutt. And Boba Fett enjoyed his work...

As they flew along in the *Falcon*, Han was wondering what to do next. He would have to find a safe place to fix his ship. Suddenly he had it.

"A buddy of mine runs a little planet around here. More like a city in the clouds, really. He won it in a card game."

"A gambler?" Leia said, frowning. "Can you trust someone like that?"

"No," Han said. "But he has no love for the Empire. I can tell you that for sure."

They neared the planet, and a police sky rover came at them. It fired in their direction.

"Your friend's a bit touchy, isn't he?" said Leia.

Han yelled into his comlink. "Hey! Tell Lando it's Han Solo here!"

At first there was no answer. Then a voice came back. "Okay. Landing platform three-two-seven."

"What did I tell you?" Han set the *Falcon* down. "Everything's going to be just fine."

Han's friend rushed up. He seemed glad to see the ex-smuggler. "How you doing, you old pirate?" he shouted with a laugh. Then he turned to the princess. "And who might you be?"

"I'm...uh, Leia."

Lando kissed her hand. "Welcome. You too, Chewie. Come on, everybody. Let me show you around my little operation here. City on top. Gas mine below. Pretty clever, huh?"

"You always were," said Han as they entered the main building. "But what does the Empire think of your mining setup?"

Lando shrugged. "You know how it is."

"Yeah. You worried about the Empire closing you down?"

"Well, to tell the truth, I was. I really was."

"So what happened?"

"Well," said Lando. "I made a deal."

He threw open a door. Waiting behind it was one of Jabba the Hutt's bounty hunters.

And Darth Vader.

Han whipped out his blaster and fired.

Vader only lifted his hand. The rays bounced away! Not even Han Solo could stand before the power of the dark side of the Force!

There was no escape.

CHAPTER EIGHT

Far away from there, Luke trembled. He had felt a disturbance in the Force. And then he had a vision of a city in the clouds.

Han was there. And he was being tortured. Leia too! She was close to death. And Threepio had been pulled apart.

Luke ran to Yoda.

The Jedi Master lowered his head. "What you see is so. But—"

"I've got to go help them!"

"No! You must finish the training. Choose not the quick and easy path, like Vader. Then you, too, will become an agent of evil!"

"They'll die if I stay here!"

The spirit of Ben Kenobi appeared beside Yoda. "Luke, this is a trap. Your friends are only the bait. It's *you* that Vader is after. He sent you this vision! You must stay here until—"

"No! I'm sorry! I have to go to them!" Luke set off for his spaceship. Then he stopped. "I'll be back. I promise. Come on, Artoo!"

"Wait!" cried Yoda. "You must listen! Blind anger...*hatred!* That is the door to the dark side!"

"Luke," called Ben. "You must not give in to it. No matter what! If you do, you'll be lost forever! Like Vader!"

"You don't have to worry!" Luke shouted back.

"Told you, I did," said Yoda to Ben. "Reckless is he. Now matters are worse."

"That boy," said Ben softly, "is our last hope."

"No," said Yoda. "There is another."

Ben Kenobi understood. There was always hope, he thought...as long as there was faith in the Force.

Luke's friends needed hope too. The terrible beatings had gone on and on. At last they stopped. And now the guards were leading them away.

Han tried to make a joke out of it. "Hey, you know what I think?" he said weakly. "We've worn these guys out."

Chewie whimpered. Leia just shrugged. Threepio was tied to the Wookiee's back. His head was on backward. He moaned.

They were taken to a large chamber.

There were metal pipes everywhere. A round platform sat in the center of the floor.

Han saw Lando standing in the shadows. The gambler looked very ashamed of himself. Han glared at him. "Is this where we get it, old buddy?"

"Listen to me, Han. Vader doesn't care about any of you. All he wants is somebody named Skywalker. And the news is the guy is on his way here now. Anyway, I'm real sorry this had to happen."

"Thanks," said Han. "You're a real pal."

"Look!" Lando cried. "Nobody's going to kill any of you!"

The bounty hunter stepped forward. "That's right, Solo," he sneered. "You're mine now. And Jabba wants you alive." He turned to the guards. "Put him into the carbon-freeze!"

Chewie suddenly found his strength. He charged the guards.

"Chewie!" Han cried as they pushed him onto the platform. "Don't do it! Take care of the princess."

Leia was crying. "I love you, Han!"

He managed to grin at her. "I know," he said.

Then the platform dropped into a pit. Burning liquid rained down on the space pilot—and froze all around him.

Darth Vader came into the chamber. "Did he survive the experiment?"

Lando checked Han. "Yes! He's in perfect hibernation."

"He's all yours, Fett," Vader told the bounty hunter. "Let the others be taken to my ship. Leave me now, all of you! The one I seek has just landed. Even now he is coming to this chamber."

CHAPTER NINE

Vader waited in silence. He drew the dark powers around him. Even the room seemed to lose its light. At last the door opened. And there he stood—the boy!

"I have been waiting for you, young Skywalker. We shall test you now."

"Good!" Luke's lightsaber flamed. He rushed at Vader.

At first the Dark Lord did not fight very hard. He merely blocked Luke's weapon with his own lightsaber. Again and again Luke lunged at him. Each time Vader turned him away.

But Luke seemed to learn with each move. He was quicker now. Stronger. The point of his sword nicked Vader's arm.

The Dark Lord stopped. "You have learned much, young one."

"You'll find that I'm full of surprises."

"And so am I."

Vader leaped at him again. With blow after blow he drove the young Jedi back. Then Luke was in a corner. There was nowhere to go. And now the Dark Lord closed in for the kill.

"You control your fear well," shouted Vader. "But to destroy me, you must release your hatred. Show it now—or die!"

Luke remembered Ben Kenobi's warning. "No!" he cried. Then he threw himself into a flip—and landed behind Vader.

The Dark Lord was caught off-guard. Luke attacked while Vader was still turning around to face him. The young Jedi's slashing lightsaber forced Vader back toward a yawning pit. As he stepped backward, Vader's foot slipped. He fell.

Luke climbed down after him. But Vader had disappeared! As Luke searched, he came to a narrow bridge over a deep, deep shaft. He crept carefully across the bridge toward the control room at its center.

Without warning Vader sprang at him. Now the Dark Lord seemed twice as powerful as before. Luke fought back bravely, but he was tiring fast.

"There is no escape!" cried Vader. He pursued Luke as the young Jedi retreated. "Don't make me destroy you. Join me and I will complete your training! Then you will know the power of the dark side."

"I will *never* join you!" Luke shouted. He tried to get away, and the Dark Lord's lightsaber lashed out once more. It sliced through Luke's right arm. Luke's hand went flying off!

Bleeding and shaking, Luke backed away. He began to pass out. Through his pain he heard Darth Vader's voice.

"Luke! You can destroy the Emperor. It is your destiny! Together we can end this war and rule the galaxy!"

"You killed my father!"

"No. I *am* your father!"

"That's not true!" Luke cried out in agony.

"Search your feelings. You know it to be true. Come with me. It is the only way!" Vader stepped closer. "Come—take my hand!"

The power of Vader's words...of Vader's

mind…were too much for the young Jedi. He knew that in another moment he would fall into the clutches of the dark side. No! It was better to fall into the pit below. Calmly, Luke let go of his hold. And down into the depths he dropped…

Was it the Force that stopped his fall? Or a mighty wind, blowing up out of the pit? Luke did not know. But something caught him and blew him against an open pipe. Then he was sucked out of the pipe. And flung into the sky! As Luke began to fall, he saw the bottom of the city. Then he saw something else. A long metal weathervane. Luke grabbed at it with his only hand. And there he clung, hoping for a miracle.

CHAPTER TEN

Luke's miracle had started earlier. It began after Han was taken away by Boba Fett. Lando and some troopers had marched Leia and Chewie toward Vader's ship. But on the way the gambler suddenly turned his guns on the troopers.

"I know what you think of me," he told Leia. "But I didn't have any choice. Come on, there's still a chance to save Han!"

They rushed to the platform where Boba

Fett's ship was docked. But they arrived too late. It was taking off!

"Let's get to the *Falcon*," said Lando.

"It doesn't have hyperdrive!" said Leia.

"Want to bet on it?" Lando grinned. "I had my people fix it."

Just then troopers came charging after them. Lando, Leia, and Chewie rushed into the *Falcon* with Artoo. Chewie started the engines. A split second later the *Falcon* blasted free.

Chewie gave a growl of relief. Then he reached for the hyperdrive controls.

But a strange feeling had come over Leia. "Wait!" she cried.

"Wait for what?" shouted Lando. "We've got TIE fighters after us!"

"I know where Luke is. We've got to go back!"

The *Falcon* made a swift turn. It raced

right past Vader's surprised fighters. "That way!" cried Leia, pointing. "There he is! He's falling! Chewie, slow down and get under him! Lando, open the top hatch!"

The *Falcon* swooped down under Luke. He dropped—right into the ship.

"Look what's happened to him!" gasped Leia. "Chewie, get me bandages. Luke, hold on until we find our transports. The medics will fix you up."

"Han?" Luke managed to whisper. "Where is he?"

"Jabba's got him."

"Don't worry about that," said Lando. "I owe him one. I'll find him. I'll get him back."

"We all will," said Luke. Then he passed out.

Chewie punched the hyperdrive. Soon they were among the other Rebel ships. The medical droids went right to work on Luke's hand. In a few days he was well again.

There was much that Leia and Luke had to do now. Together they would plan the rescue of Han. And the return of the Jedi.

But that is another story.

Larry Weinberg has been both a lawyer and a playwright, but now spends almost all of his time writing for children. He is also a devoted Star Wars fan and has seen each of the Star Wars movies so many times that he's lost count. Among his many books are *Star Wars: The Making of the Movie; Guess a Rhyme; Frankenstein;* and *Dragonslayer: The Storybook Based on the Movie.*

Mr. Weinberg lives in Woodstock, New York.

Continue the fight against the Empire in the next book from the Classic Star Wars® trilogy:

RETURN OF THE JEDI™

The Emperor stopped in front of Darth Vader. "Rise, my friend. I would talk to you," he said.

"The Death Star will be finished in time, my master," said Darth Vader in his deep voice.

"I know," said the Emperor. "You have done well. Now you wish to seek young Skywalker."

"Yes, my master."

"You need not hurry. In time he will seek you. Then you must bring him before me. He has grown strong. Only together can we turn him to the dark side of the Force."

The Emperor laughed softly. "Everything is going just as I have planned. Just as I have seen. Soon, Skywalker will be with us, and the Rebellion will be no more!"